# The Adventures of
# Porridge Oats

*Grange Calveley*
Creator of Roobarb and Custard

© 2016 Grange Calveley

# The Real Dinosaur

Written and drawn by Grange Calveley

(Inspired by my grandchildren)

© 2017 Grange Calveley

It was Tuesday. Porridge had slept at Dan and Tom's house on the other side of the stream. At George and Emily's house the munching and crunching of breakfast was really loud.

"I wonder if Porridge and the kids are awake yet?" said Emily, as the kitchen door opened with a crash and Porridge Oats and cousins Dan and Tom tumbled into the house – all ready to play.

With breakfast over and the sun in the sky the children and Porridge set out towards Meeting Spot Tree where they sometimes plan their adventures.

The adventure meetings were always the same; the kids could never decide on anything. Porridge Oats was always asked if he could come up with an idea for the day. He always did.

"Mmm … now, let me think before my brain explodes," thought Porridge. Then … "Ahaa!" He announced that he knew where there was a real dinosaur.

"There are no dinosaurs any more," said Tom.

"Well, there is *one*!" said Porridge.

"Prove it," said Emily.

"I *can* prove it," announced Porridge Oats. "Follow me," he cried and the children followed, laughing and chortling that there was no such thing as a real dinosaur any more.

Through the wood the children followed along like a little band of explorers; giggling amongst themselves about what Porridge might say when he couldn't find his dinosaur.

Along the way, Porridge came up with the idea of making a mud dam in the stream. Later, they played on the old tyre swing and then they dug up their buried treasure to see if it was still there; all Porridge's ideas – all time wasting activities.

"I know why Porridge is coming up with all these ideas," said George. "He doesn't want us to get to wherever it is we are going; because there is no dinosaur." "You are right," said Emily while the others agreed; but on they went.

Suddenly, Porridge Oats stopped. "From now on I want you all to be very quiet," he whispered before moving on with the others tip toeing along behind - as quiet as field mice.

Eventually, the little band of explorers came to the edge of the wood. Porridge turned and whispered 'stop' and everyone fell into a heap with lots of laughing. "Quiet *please*!" Porridge whisper-shouted and all was silent - except for Dan's hic-up!

"There," said Porridge proudly and the children all looked on in silence. "That's farmer Tweedtrouser's horse!" scoffed Emily. "Not!" Porridge replied firmly. "That's a *real* dinosaur; look at its spikes!" he whispered and the children shuffled uneasily.

"Stop it!" said Dan. "I'm scared. "Me too," said George just as the monster snorted and everyone screamed, even Porridge, as they turned and ran until they all crashed into the safety of the kitchen at Dan and Tom's house.

"DINOSAUR!" The children shouted before explaining, one by one; "Massive!" ... "Monster!" ... "Teeth!" ... "And spikes!" ... "And ... a *really scary* SMOKY ROAR!" they yelled as one voice.

Dan and Tom's mum smiled and said they could all watch <u>one</u> TV show before teatime; adding that she thought that they *may* find it interesting.

Porridge and the kids dived onto the carpet in the lounge and, at that very moment, a dinosaur film began. "Wow! How cool is that?" said Tom.

"Was it really, really a real dinosaur today," Emily whispered into Porridge's ear but he didn't answer - just in case Dan and Tom's mum might hear him talking.

Do you believe that Porridge Oats
discovered a real dinosaur?

**The Adventures of Porridge Oats** by Grange Calveley, Creator of Roobarb and Custard

- One: The Great Storm
- Two: The Real Dinosaur
- Three: The Giant Snowdog
- Four: The Witch's House
- Five: Mrs Rumbletumble's Umbrella
- Six: The Good Fun Circus

Six little books to collect

Find my books @ grangecalveley.com

Printed in Great Britain
by Amazon